TO THE WONDERS OF NATURE THAT ETERNALLY INTRIGUE ME,
THE ADONIS` THAT MAKE MY HEART BEAT WILDLY, AND ALL
THE SWEET SOULS WHO INSPIRE ME,

THIS BOOK IS FOR YOU.

L. Pettit

GW00468159

Cover Illustration by Louisa Charrington.

To John
Thankyou for your
friendship
Leigh

1.

Poetry is the spontaneous overflow of powerful feelings :
It takes its origin from emotion recollected in tranquility .

- William Wordsworth

There is pleasure in the pathless woods, There is rapture in
the lonely shore
There is society where none intrudes , by the deep sea and music
in its roar,
I love not man the less but nature more .

-Lord Byron

2.

Table Of Contents

Leukothea

My eyes awash in a blur of grey as light rains filter through the Psamma
Petrichor bluffs its way into my senses
 As the surf crashes beyond the dunes

I walk a steady mile the sand gives way under my feet
The waves rolling away into the sea Then back to stroke my toes
The gentle winds soothe my soul as sea monsters fight to the death beneath
Amongst the tomb of Amphitrite
I can hear the roars and the clashing of steel
As the sea batters at the shore
And I so dream of being amongst the battles
Fins and tentacles and menacing eyes
 As they glint in the blackened brine

I sit amongst bleached Driftwood as the sun reveals her golden smile
To be shunned by the Behemoth of all storms
 His black cloak fills the skies
And the battles rage all the more
And I sit and I wait for the beast to emerge

As I glance at my feet where my tail of turquoise pearls should be
I cry salty tears that fill the ocean blue
The fins and the tentacles and the eyes of black seek out the source of the
silent plea
As the watchtower light Steers ships in the night

Leviathan pulls me in to the Place I belong
 And I find my Fins my Gills and my song.

5.

CARPE NOCTEM

Let us seize the night
Kiss the moonbeams from my lips
Let us sit upon the black rocks by the bay Wrapped in each others silky
nakedness As the moored boats rock themselves to sleep
The quiet melody of the sea

The witching hours are for the lovers
The dreamers
These who believe in magic
 Who cast the spell of passion as their bodies meet under the moon
The herald of the night

Your hands trace every inch of me As my tongue traces every inch of you
The groove of our pulses unify
My hips mimic the ebb and flow of the tide Gaining momentum as storms
arise
Great rods of lightning sent from the gods surge as you enter me
I feel every blazing thrust

The diaphanous haze of early light illuminates your splendour and I am in
awe of you,
your aura,
 your touch
You energise me with the tips of your fingers
And the feel of your breath on my neck
Take me again at the crescendo of the dawn.

INNSAEI

I want to wear the ocean like a soft summer dress
That flows with the wind as it hugs my smooth limbs
Sparkling blues whites and turquoise of the swell and the sea foam
As the crashing sounds burn my heart with joy
Our hair tangles in the breeze
And you twist your fingers around mine

As the crashing waves gift us sharks teeth and pearls
From their jade palace in the deep
And the sirens song travels to our fated ears
You are my Anchor
My raison d`etre

As the lust melts from your lips to mine
The forsythia blossom sun slowly fades
And the scent of blooming wild flowers remain
As I breathe you in
The evocative scent of your skin unleashes the wildness in me
And the feeling of home all at once

This, an Elysian dream I wish to return to always
As your mirage shimmers upon the Marmaris
The the taste of you upon my lips
I wade deep
my exalted soul seeps into the drink

My blissful intentions of an aequorial farewell .

SLEEPER

Where the tracks meet The fork in the line dwindles this way and that
Whispered memories of lost souls travelling nowhere
And those who's lives were forsaken
The escape of a harsh reality
As the leaves scatter in the breeze they remember the girl
With the pale eyes And the sad smile And the heart that beat with
unrequited intensity
So easily forgotten as a passing storm
Yet the wind reminisces how she took to the sky like dandelion clocks

The bits between coloured the tracks in splashes of cyan Clashing with the
steely sleepers
As the white clouds became heavy and grey shedding a tear for the girl
without a name
A flesh that tastes so sour
marinaded in destitute dreams

little speckled eggs nestle within silk spun tresses
Like silver bells chiming in the light of spring
As forest dwellers seek out the sweetest of Scents
They taste her sorrow upon their lips
The ticket stub set free from her grasp continued it's journey along the
track

Nowhere to go and no way back.

LULLABY

The empty page draws me in
 It's like me but on paper
All the empty spaces In my heart and my arms
The spaces around me
My bed
On my lips
Between my legs
 Between my fingers
I want to curl myself around a person
My person
Burn the kitchen down in our passion
Forget the pans are boiling over

Walk through night forests listening to the sounds only heard by the light
of the moon
when all is still
Lay between tall grasses in the most comfortable silences
broken only by a kiss as crickets serenade us
Count the stars
pick out the prettiest brightest lights that pierce the dark veil between us
and the heavens

Make sweet music, the melodies between the sheets
the moans, the sounds of our hearts pounding in our chests
The delicate chime of sweat prickling our skin
Cutting through the quiet of the room
Making a ruckus and bathing in the orgasmic glow afterwards

Its the magic that calms the hurricane
 lulling it till its little more than a summers breeze
That strokes our skin as we bathe under the sun between the dunes and the
rock pools.

Summanus God of nocturnal thunder bring me the most beautiful dreams
Fill my heart with light
Scatter my lips with the kiss of cosmic dust.

SWEET SORROW

Sacred Selene, Maiden of the moon
I ask of you ,where is the love I seek
Is it that I have simply not earned it
Through all the lives I have lived

Can it be so

Is it that my scars thought to be buried away are visible to all but myself
Great slashes across my heart
Jagged scars adorn my limbs
Like lightning bolts decorating my delicate flesh
Deep gouges in my eyes
metallic scarlet jewels taint my cheeks
Do my lips speak the unspeakable
Does the sorrow of me flow from my veins ,a river so sombre that no one
dare cross

My heart is still full, It beats like yours
My hands are soft and warm
I hold the summers breeze upon my fingertips
They yearn the familiar warmth of tenderness and intimacy
As do my eyes
oh! to gaze upon the most perfectly imperfect human
and still my oculi of sapphires will be filled with awe

Glimmering lights explode in my irises upon meeting his gaze
Sweet sweet supernova
To mirror that in return
a waking dream
Let me sleep
Deep beautiful dreams of the most delicate of all kisses

Trees rustle in the winds of my mind as they stir my thoughts
Alive with the hum of all the smallest creatures of the earth
The insignificant
Love is all this and more
It is creation
Evolution

the end of all things in one.

OCEAN SIGH

The palms wave farewell to the last of the golden sun
Lovers Driftwood hideaways perch upon the escarpment
passion is caught on the breeze rustling through the grass

Then…

settling upon the wings of doves
Soaring and plunging
The moans and the gasps play on the wind
I could die a thousand times with a kiss from adonis' lips

I choose death

Sublime momentary bliss fleeting yet perpetual
The sand buries my feet each ebb of the sea caresses my skin
And I sink deeper into the lustful ocean
The sand and the salt and the taste of him

the wetness within gushes with intensity
Deep throbs remain in my loins Amongst the waves
As he sleeps
I am drenched in anticipation as he stirs with the wind and the heat of the
fire
And the sounds of the waves crash in my belly with each stroke of his
powerful body
And I die over and over in the most delicious way

He brings me to life with a smile that could sink ships
As maidens steer towards the rocks transfixed
By the man with the mane
And a spirit untamed
As he rocks me again and again upon the beach with no name
And ill visit this place till I breathe my last
and I'll smell him in the air
and smile with my heart.

SHINRIN YOKU

Over bridges and fields I roam
Until I reach the place my heart Longs for
I breathe in the air, it feels like magic
The forest Bath soaks me in its tranquility
The euphonious creaks and groans as the trees bend with the wind
welcome me home
The Scents of pine and ferns warm my soul

I sit in the dirt

Watching the ants clamber over little stones
They must feel mountainous to these tiny beings
They make me feel like a giant

Then I look up

I am drowned by the great oaks and I am reminded of my small stature
An insignificant speck
Thinking about the universe and its endlessness makes me feel smaller still
But here in my secret place I feel all my worries dissipate
like snowflakes on a warm tongue

The sun sprinkles scintillas of gold through the gaps in the sky of leaves
All the greens
Sparkling emerald hues
I feel As if the roots of the trees are trying to feel their way around me
To unearth parts of myself long hidden
As I tell them tales of old
All the tears I've shed,
Smiles I've beheld
And hearts I've cherished.

ABYSSOPELAGIC HONEYMOON

The ocean
how I love the majesty of her
The surface opalescent, Iridescent
Light bounces on the ripples like magic
Beneath the beauty An obscured treachery
Standing at the edge of a hidden abyss you feel the pull
Intriguing depths imploring you to discover them
Amphitrite calls your name amongst the crashing waves
Her sweet voice carries to the shore

"Dive in! swim and swim till your breath escapes you "
She draws you in with siren like hypnosis
Then keeps you for herself

A cleptomania of mortal ruin

You shall not see light again
Nor breathe the air
Your Skeletal remains become part of the ocean floor
You bleed out a beacon of scarlet
The fish pick at your eyes and nestle inside your rib cage
Eels slither around your skull
Swirling around and around where your brain should be

You always loved the ocean
Eternal matrimony with the sacred waters
Till death do you part.

PARAPHILIA

Synergy surges through every sinew of my flesh
The moment of divine unity, our bodies becoming one
My skin is alive with the electricity of your touch
The sensation of a million drops of dew exploding within the most magical
of all the woodland realms
Can be felt so long after
The wild flames of our souls burn hot with desire

I could fall into your Luciferian eyes if i were to allow it,
Draw me in deeper and deeper if you will it so

The alignment of the stars on this night of our embrace
As the merging of celestial bodies rhyme with our own
The universe commands us

Apollos silver bow pierces our hearts
Wounds that will never heal
The pain of love is too pleasurable to deny

Sado-Masochism tends to my needs
 more so than pretty bows and violets in bloom

Yet i still desire to smell the sweetness
For just a moment

And still my immortality is a delicious curse
One i shall not regret until my soul becomes weary
And i have explored every whim
And only then i shall feel punished by this transformation i imposed upon
myself.

WILD HORSES

Humans, we whelve our secrets
Hidden away in old trunks of worn leather
Locked tight with intricate keys
In the attic Whispering in the gloom
I have seen and done some dark things
Things that should be lost at sea

Yet they faintly linger
I no longer run from the torment and vexation
Rather I face it head on
The roots of my conviction grounded deep
And roar like the Heathen woman I am

Write them down in black, all of it every last word then tear that paper into
tiny pieces and scatter the air like mardi gras bunting

Naked and unashamed
I am a powerful femme
Sexual
Energetic
Unapologetic

Still I have my secrets
They're right here on the tip of my tongue
Peppering my lips like sweet sugar cane
Yet stinging like an Absinthe kiss

I have learnt to tame the whirlpool of swirling Obsidian
like a gentle Iroquois woman would a wild mustang

A faithful companion with a free spirited soul.

AWAKEN THE GIRL

Show me the open road
Not a soul For miles
Just waves of heat on the blacktop
Making all in the periphery shimmer Like a serendipitous portal
Take my hand ,lead me down twisty shingle paths
To secret beaches and coves
Our feet sink into the golden grains
Sargassum floats atop the calm
My hair is salt tousled and sun bleached
Peppered sunlight across my cheeks like rosy pink apples
As I rub the sand from my eyes phosphenes dance their pretty dance like
fireflies

My Thalassophilic tendencies would have me stay for eternity
Combing the beach for star fish and tiny gleaming shells
Bathing in the waters then drying my soft wet body on warm rocks
My eyes of blue gaze up at the endless sky
As clouds pass over driven like the sails of a ship in high winds
 Eos rises into the sky from her oceanic slumber
Bringing the beauty of dawn over the murmuring waves
I do not need books or art

Not in this moment
The ocean and her breathtaking energy is all I need
The way the waters lap gently at the shore
I too gently sway and smile and sing

For this is paradise.. this is everything.

THE COLOUR OF RAIN

The rain battered my roof with thunderous applause
As I lay in my darkened room upon feather down
I can smell the freshness of it
Feel the synergy of the Gods in the air
As the rumble of wild horses spreads across the blackened skies

Crows caw and take flight
Seeking shelter from the rage of the Anemoi
The swirling inky sky holds a malevolence
Sheets of rain drown the valleys
And in this moment naked and free
I step out of the comfort of my bed
And into the cold needles falling from the menacing nimbus
The leaves dance as the shards of Crystal water hits

Hues of midnight blue and the deepest onyx
Against the emerald green of the trees
All the colours blur as I shower in the icy downpour
I close my eyes
The water runs the length of my bare slenderness
Lashing at my nudity
Joining the sapphire river at my feet
The freedom and fragility of my wet skin and naked soul

The salacious tension of the storm ridden air Liberates me with fierce
intensity
Uncaged
Untethered

My tears, a pool of pure bliss.

BLOOM

Let's stay here, till the rising of the sun
Secure in Our blanket Fort
Talk about what's hurt us the most
Unravel the intricacies of our minds

Let us heal together
Place your hand in mine As I trace the lines with my fingertips

My soul is old, older than this earth
But my heart is young filled with hope
Place your trust in me
I give to you the purest form of love

Unconditionally.

SHIBARI

The rope burns me with such exquisite tenderness
Red lines around my throat and wrists
Pull them tighter

Just a little

Bind me with intricate knots
wind them around my waist and thighs
Till you hear the gasp
And I fall into the rabbit hole of bliss
Down deeper and deeper into the glorious depths

My tantalised lips tingle
Awaiting your kiss of life As I rouse from this little death
I smell your sweat on my skin and in my hair
It arouses me like an elixir laced with aphrodisia
I melt onto you as you melt into me

Your eyes of the lightest jade speak more to me than words
An ineffable language only lovers can hear
Hold me tight till I can barely breathe
As I kiss you with all the fire of Hephaestus
The raging inferno of the Olympian hearth is no match for our passion.

MORTE

As I sleep in this, my eternal slumber
Wipe the tears from your cheek
My body will wither and vanish
But my soul will be here
Speak to me in your dreams
I'll be there

As the earth consumes my physical form
The sounds of my voice will remain
Hear it in the wind and the waves
That's where I'll be

These eyes, though dull and lifeless
My energy and spark reside in the stars
Look up at the night sky and see me shine

I'll never be gone while you still think of me.

KING OF WOLVES.

The fire in the sky

A mere echo of my heart
Be still my love Let me coat your wounds with my kisses
Your battle scarred flesh
Delicious Vermillion gushes onto my sweet lips
Bury yourself in the warmth of my bosom

My wild wolf

The ravages of war still surge through your veins Like molten lava
An ancient volcano long inactive now unleashed by the Gods themselves

your passion burns into me
 I take both the pleasure and pain willingly
The last of your seed coats my porcelain skin
Dark ashen Furs surround our Heady Union
I have waited many a long night for this moment
My fair locks and your dark mane tangle around our flesh Prickled with
beads of salty dew

as the dawn of a new day cracks through the dark
The battle field beyond awash with the remains of our enemies
Carrion descendsPicking clean the bones
They praise the killer wolf for this gift

Their wings mimic the fire in our bellies
Like a cauldron of bats.

ICARUS

Your lips blister as they touch the Fiery wrath that lies between my thighs
As the heat and destruction spreads with pyromanias glee
The pain peaks pleasure
Your irises alight, deep blood Red As they meet the fire in mine
Destroy the fabric that bonds me in modesty
Tear each thread,
Unravel me
Scars of wax slip down my flesh Hitting your tongue like a pounding drum
Drowning out the timbre of our hearts

Every muscle and sinew of you crushes me till I cannot breathe
I feel the stars aglow and the black waves crashing in the deep
Our blood flows with passionate rage
Till you are part of me and I you

Satiate me with your sweat
Cover me with warm amazonian rain
Swimming in you Like underwater Caves
An abyss of sensual bliss
The haunting dark that draws me deep
And keeps me.

MOTHER

Blood washes over the sultry sky
Malevolent clouds black as coal skim the horizon
Heavy with complacency
Full of pain
Blackened decay and rivers of red scour the landscape
Crimson roses in the breeze
The Theoi Meteoroi bring the storm
Dashes of light streak through the skyline
Deep chasms appear between the Heavens and Hades gate
Anguish drowns the earth once more
Synonymous of the lucid tears of a mother and her dying child

All is dark. All is still as Cybele sighs her last.

LIBERTAS

What's in a name? A jumble of letters
We answer to it just the same
Belonging is the nemesis of loneliness
The spark of recognition to a familiar voice satisfies the child inside
yet,If I had no name would it make me less of a person?

I think Not

I taste of fire and brimstone With a wildlings heart
I could walk from one forest to the next my feet raw and bloodied
and still not feel satisfied
I need to see and to be
Do not attempt to clip my wings
I am not meant to be caged

I want to Crawl on all fours to my lovers bed and lick him awake
Claim animalistic passion
then leave the sheets messy

My shadow at sunset disappears into the haze of orange and red
And I shall be gone
remembered as just a frantic tumultuous dream.

ERIS

Tiny Iridescent bubbles
Candlelight casting an amber glow upon her skin
As she immerses herself in the warm bath
Her hair shimmers in the water like golden shoals
She reads tales of Gods and Goddesses
Ancient shrines and new moon rituals
Her heart filled with wonder

She closes her eyes
Drifting into a haze of fantasies To faraway worlds and magical lands
where she will be queen Wild and untamed
A ruler who will ride out to battle
Blade at the ready

Fierce

Her crown of rare gems atop her lustrous curls
An Empress who seduces Kings and men
Then slays the unworthy
She is both powerful and terrifying
Queen of death and beauty

Now awake from her dream
Candles snuffed
The scent of wax, jasmine and starflower
Water tepid, bubbles long diminished

Just a girl Yet Queen of her own castle.

BEACH COMBING

A wildness subdued
As the waves kiss the shore
Washed up samphire swims around our feet
As we walk the bed of shingle and seashells
Long abandoned by their inhabitants
Apollo hides his warmth behind the clouds touching us with his rays
Golden shimmers dance on our bare skin
The salty taste on your lips excites my soul
Sitting in the breeze against the velvety comfort of you

The waves ripple on the surface of the silky aquamarine sheet of the ocean
The magic that lies beneath we can only imagine
Upon nightfall we walk to the edge
Our skin free from the confines of the fabric we previously bore

The purity of our naked bodies, our souls undressed
Our hearts full as we walk deeper into this Atlantian realm together
We are unaffected by the glacial waters
The heat of our bodies keeps the chill from reaching our bones
Fireside heat stokes the flames in our bellies
Igniting dormant passions
As you lay me upon the soft sand and enter my body and mind

Our skin etched with the shimmering salty grains
The rush of lust amongst the dunes
Mimics the swell of the tide
Rising
Falling
Rushing
Crashing
Crescending against the rocks
Visceral, Wild and Free.

FROSTBITE

My lips are cold
Ice blue tinged with indigo
the surface of the Crystal glass lake
Transparent
Cracks appear like manzanita branches
I wish to plunge into the bitter depths
Where the fish are suspended animation
Awaiting spring thaw
And Jack frost sketches snowflakes
The wild wind bites
A searing pain on my cheeks
It is beautiful yet Treacherous
The blanket of snow like a feather bed
A dream you'd not awaken from

Boreas the bringer of winter is near
I feel him in my bones.

HEARTS SONG

The sun spins gold in my eyes of blue
Your lips speak the words of a love so true
Take my hand in this Meadow of white
As we lay entangled awaiting the night

Your Lust is unleashed
Like a Ravenous Beast
How the heat of your kiss
Burns my hips
Our souls unite an unbreakable tether
If only this embrace could last forever

Alas is the time to say farewell
Here I shall wait under your spell
With a heavy heart and empty arms
I pray you have not come to harm

I will wait a thousand turning tides
As I search for my love in the darkest of skies.

LA DOULEUR EXQUISE

My Love is the kind that burns the soul
And you are so Blissfuly unaware
How the colours of the sunset wash through me
And the stars light your very eyes

I could swim to the ocean Bed
Just to touch you for a moment
Risk the crushing deep for one kiss

To feel your hands on my waist
Leaving imprints on my flesh

That I shall cherish till my final Breath.

PEACE

The tears that fall are not from pain or anguish
Every lucent drop is my story
Every thing my eyes beheld
The facets of a lifetime
Delicate levaliers

Look deep into my soul
And you shall see mirrored gems full of wonder and light
With darkness in-between
Vengeful words left unsaid
A poison chalice I dare not sip from
For the delicious liquid would be my undoing
The way it would desire to infect my spirit

I transcend space and time to a higher state of consciousness
It resonates in my bones, in every atom

I am a Goddess

Eirene incarnate
I harbour no anger
It leaves me the way the Redwings fly south for Winter

Seeking warmer climes
I drift away upon the breeze a smile upon my lips
Like autumnal leaves following the stream.

ALI' IKAI

Rock formations overlook the sea
They look like giants in shadow
My bare sandy feet reach the very edge
My toes of mother of pearl catch the light just right
I am not oblivious to the risk
I know if I leap now I may wash up on unchartered shores a lifeless ghost
Or I may plunge into the cool blue swell and experience the heights of enchantment
I accept the fate that shall befall me

It is in the hands of the Deivės Valdytojos
The weavers of time and fate with the threads of human lives

My dress of turquoise billows in the wind imitative of the waves
I so desperately desire them to wash away my sins
Grant me absolution
Trinkets of coral adorn my fingers clasped in rose gold

The early light lustre bounces on the waves
Like a thousand shoals of silver jewelled fish
I breathe in the sweet air
The faint scent of coconut and hibiscus flowers fills my bronzed nose
Kissed by the sun Scattered with light freckles
The fine fair hairs on my arms look like glitter as solaris smiles high in the sky

I hear the giants in the rocks grumbling to each other
I close my eyes

And I let myself fall.

OPUS

At dusk when all is still
In foetal like comfort I am lost in the pages of books
Cloth covered and leather bound gateways
In this silent solitude

Before long the ink blurs with my lonely tears
And the pages become a mass of black
Creeping death
Fallow deers graze I go unnoticed
As though I'm not bothersome to the gentile and content
The whites of my eyes mimic the waxing moon
And I question wether I am even real

All the sky is full of glitter
It seems Infinitely bigger once the twilight hours descend
I should like to sit up there with Jupiter and Saturn
And ask them if they can see me
And await their answer my heart beating wildly

To be met with silence.

THE LOVERS.

Into the deep where dreams are made,
In your dark eyes I shall bathe
Out of my body my soul will wander
Amidst thoughts of wanton hunger

The astral light from which I ride
Casts upon this unholy night
Mother moons steely gaze
Our souls entwined a lustful haze
Our blood runs hot surging through our veins
The devil shalt not speak our names

For we the sinners so set upon
Twin flames becoming one.

BEACH GOTHS AND GRANOLA

The endless ocean
Cool crystal waters lapping against our smooth wet skin
Sun beams dancing on the ripples of the aquamarine eiderdown
Scoop me into your arms
Place your lips on mine till I lose myself in you,
Until it feels as though we are alone in the universe.

Perching on the warm rocks,
Sandy limbs,
Wet hair
Kiss me more till the moon shines its ethereal glow upon the still waters
Mars
Venus
The plough
Let's gaze at the stars and talk about life
Fireside warmth, little Sparks rise up amidst the smoke of our
beach rescued log
We could stay forever
Pretend this doesn't have to end
I can be a mermaid, you an Adonis
Claim the rocks as ours
Defend them from the sea urchins and the gulls.

ECHO

She was just an echo of everything that once was
The waves crashing on the stony shore
The last bird song
A lovers kiss
She whispered in the Caves
Her delicate voice disappearing into the nothing
The sound of the rain on the narcissi
Like little chimes made by elves
Silver rays of moon shine cast upon the stillness

The blackness of her subterranean lair seemed to swallow her voice
If not for the Stalagtites of pure white selenium her pretty songs would
drift away

All the magic of the world slipped from her lips
Pure golden light shone from her heart
She sent it into the world from the darkness in which she dwelled

One day she would be free
Escaping upon the wings of a hummingbird into the night sky
where her velvet tones would echo for eternity
But for now just an echo in the dark
Just an echo

Echo

Echo.

LOVERS GAZE

Meet me under the full moon
On a cold stark winters night
Bat's flutter amidst the lunar light
They swim through the torrents of air
Weightless and free

An eerie light is cast upon the frozen lake
A surface of bevelled crystal glass
Shadows dance around us as the breeze catches the evergreens
Scents of cedar and campfires play on the wind

Pull me close
Your warm breath on my neck
Your lips brand me with their heat
I am yours
And you are mine

Trace my heart with your fingers
Undress my soul
Layers of deep crimson velvet
As i bear all to you my twin flame
You are the light to my dark
The moon to my tide.

AEGEON & CETO

You turn me inside out
Your death stare stops my heart in its tracks like a derailed train
A consequence of disaster ,unstoppable until impact
Then in the midst of the chaotic confusion
Bouncing rays fill my eyes
Like a giddy child disembarking a carousel
I am swimming in a sea of infatuation
Buoyantly upheld

Slide your tongue across my throat then tear out my jugular with your teeth
Rose red gushes
It is a love that destroys but I need it
I thirst for the pain of desire
Every inch of my yearning flesh cries out
Little currents of electricity reach every nerve
From the tips of your fingers to the small of my back

Now in the shallows away from harm
Where you hold me gently and stroke my soul
And the waves of bliss lap at our tongues
Before Charybidis summons storms and whirling pools
That drag me under where I cannot breathe
Discarding me on the sun scintilla`d shore leaving me yearning for more

All the bruises of ripened fruits scatter across my skin
Add to the charm
And you reel me in again and again.

SOMNIUM

Take me away to a magical place
Where the stars are always alight
Where the trees bough and sigh as if they're alive whispering their inner
most secrets
Where the crystal clear lake filters through the rocks like molten silver
And the moon smiles upon us.
Where mystical creatures roam
Winged horses and tiny sea dragons
A place where everything smells like freshly cut grass and Geranium
blossoms
And the cotton candy clouds sail across the night sky.

We can lay together hand in hand
In this perpetual twilight
Naming the stars
Chiron, Dionysus and Demeter
After the Gods of the wandering planets,
Let us never wake from this enchanted place
Midnight orchids surround us
Their tendrils Wrap around our limbs
Pulling us into the earth
Little jewelled beetles scuttle around us
Rubies emeralds and sapphires

The under place, cool and echoey
Caves where the silk worms spin their precious threads
the weavers of dreams
With time we accept the tomb in which we will reside
Eternally
Peacefully
Memories of the world above fade
Our bodies nourish the roots of the mighty Oak trees

Our souls bud and bloom in the spring.

DEEP SWIM

I ache for that black sea
The darkest depths unseen
I ache for The way it gushes around our naked flesh
The hour of midnight all is pitch
the deepest hues and I see nothing but you
An infinity of dark surrounds us
As the waves lick us
Till we are shoulder deep and
The shingle finds its home between our toes

The stars in the night sky seek us out
As we climb the steep path by the beach this balmy night
To slip between white cotton sheets
The moans cut through the rush of calm
And I feel your heat as i boil Over
And over
And over

We sleep content and satiated
I melt into your body till the sun peeks over the horizon
As your lips find their way across and under my skin
You are under my skin
Close the door and walk the hall

I'll still want you again

And again.

HOURGLASS

Upon the quickening of my heart
And the maddening of mind
I search the endless darkness of my soul
Wading through the streams of acrid tears
I want nothing of material wealth
But that first pang of love
Prickling the flesh of my entire being

The anticipation, the knot in my stomach As my head swims with thoughts
of you
The coming days feel like another eternity
The hands of the clock seem to slow the more I look at them
The hour glass and its grains of sand fall in such slow motion
I feel they are suspended in mid air as if by magic
I crave you
Your touch
Your Ravenous lips upon mine
The sound of your breath against my ear
The way it hushes my terror
Calms the raging horses inside
As our bodies writhe and gleam in the Candlelight
The vitriolic sweat that falls from your brow Burning my eyes
Yet borne of passion
The salty sting is Beautifully delicious

Then

The rise and fall of your chest as you sleep
I lie awake breathing you in
Lost in the afterglow
I am nothing If just a wick awaiting your spark

Twin flames apart are just a mere fluttering of warmth.

KAILANI

The ocean calls my name
The syllables flutter on the waves And in the wind
The cool waters lap against my skin
Purifying my soul
Clothes discarded on the sandy shore

Immersing myself I lay back and trust the waters to hold me
I float weightlessly looking up at the sky
Blue grey Dotted with sea birds
The September sun warms me a little
The sun gods casting their love upon me
Apollo and Freyr
Head first I plunge into the unknown
Deeper and deeper into Oceana
Turquoise like my eyes but deeper

So much deeper

Shoals of fish surround me
Their scales a shimmer of light
Silver and gold
Treasures of the deep

My hair long and fine trails behind me Mermaid like
I feel alive
Coming up for air before returning to the place I love most

Queen of Atlantis.

TENDERNESS.

I've suffered many losses
I've forgotten what having something feels like
Having someone to wipe away my tears
The sorrowful ones and those induced by laughter and joy
To kiss me goodnight as the stars wink at us
Choose our favourite foods in the grocery store Then cook together in our
underwear
To wake up beside a warm body
That ravishes me morning noon and night
Someone to talk about life with
All the things we love about the world
Everything that scares us
And all the magic we dream of

I miss those things

More so I want to tenderly kiss away Their tears
Wake them in the still of the night with the intensity of my passion
Be their pillow when they need comfort
And their light in dark places.

SANGUIS LUCIFERA

Here I lie betwixed the bones
From these sinful lips thou shalt hear the moans

Sanguine slews upon this ritual knife
Eye for an eye life for a life

As the crimson dreams run from their slits
Drip drip drip as the sorrow hits

And I lap at their wounds upon this ground
My bloodied tongue slides around and around

Till all is supped and I lay fulfilled
Before the day breaks more blood shalt be spilled.

DWELL.

Find me in the forests
My laughter in the wind
Free as a lark
My bare feet against the mossy ground
Prickled with thorns
Flowers tousled in my hair

Tresses of woven gold

My cabin is Nestled deep in the Pines
Away from the world, the people and their pollution
Where I write songs for the birds
And pick flowers for the goddess Artemis
My dress of silk snags against the trees

The beauty of imperfection

I shall stay here forever till all that remains are memories of me carried on
Birdsong
And the wood nymphs will tell the little nymphs the legend of the lady of
the forest

And they will call me Gaia.

EROTICRYPTICA.

The glacial air of the cemetery chills our bones
On this winters eve
An icy breeze flows past us Like sheets of cool mulberry silk
Nocturnal souls hide amidst the foliage,
Their eyes fixed upon the scene their lips tinged with blood
The electricity in the air shimmers its lucent haze
Stars above shine like little diamonds against the deep dark sky
Cetacean blue velvet billows as the twinkling nightlights scatter their glow
Lighting our way
The crescent moon peeps out from behind the ancient ruins
Her silent gaze watches over us

Goddess Khiones icy fingers creep along our naked flesh
Blissfully inebriated in each others scent and the sweet taste of merlot on
our lips
Ancient weathered tombs orbit our ritualistic setting
My lovers pounding heat Between my thighs
His back against the frozen ground glancing up at the twilight canopy
As shooting stars skim the sky
Pirates graves and dead man's fingers
The deathly blooms of White roses wilt in their wintry grave
Bodies merging in the open air
In this otherworldly passion there are only two
Our souls ignite billowing auburn flames
Prophecies fulfilled,
Written in the stars by ancient sky mariners
Burned into the pages of time.

UNREQUITED.

Beneath the stars
The sapphire blanket
I lay here upon the mountains and think of you
Where are you now
Are you thinking of me
Or am I a faint memory
Drifting away
The way the sand drifts during a storm
Scattered everywhere yet nowhere at all
Tiny fragments amounting to nothing

Or could it be you do think of me
Thoughts like billowing flames
Plumes of smoke rising between the trees
For all to see
Wearing your heart on your sleeve
Yet I am blind to it all

Faint hints like delicate petals elude me.

EVE.

The blades of insomnia cut through my eyelids
I am forced awake
The restless undead
I taste the bitter dew of fear on my lips

Black rose petals fall in curtains as I lay chained to my bed
Paralysis triumphantly holding me prisoner
As the roses transform into tiny screeching demons
That mean to take over my mind And rupture my soul with their bloody
nihilism

There is little need for greed
I shall survive on scraps
The morsels of love you tease me with nourish me more than a debauched
banquet
I yearn to dream
Yet I reside in this unending carousel of sleeplessness

I have but torn every hair from my own head
In a desperate attempt to feel something other than this
What is this I speak of?
It is the black door closing shut
The garden of Eden beyond
where all is lush and Temptation is rife
It is the feel of Beelzebubs breath on my neck as I am pulled into the dark
Chained tortured and scorned till the buds of my heart wither and die

The screw in my skull twists tighter and tighter till I bleed visions of you
onto the floor
Cerberus laps at the gore and I pet his matted coat
I wait in vain for you to rescue me and take me back to our garden
The apples have fallen they rot with disease and decay

You aren't Coming are you? You never were.

FOOLS GOLD.

Who should be so fickle as a magpie and it's treasures
Upon seeing something that possesses more sparkle
For the sun casts light for the giddy at heart
Whereas the darkness reveals true beauty
It's easy to adore a sun-drenched jewel
But to see a glimmer of light in a dark heart

That's real.

PAPILLON.

Loneliness
I feel I am quite the scholar on the subject
Describing it should come naturally
Yet how do you put into words
That feeling in your stomach
It's physical
Like an ache that won't go away
The swirling void in an empty pit
Your ears echo with tinnitus Whispering then screeching
Tear ducts full
They brim over except they have nowhere to go
No one to catch them as they fall
Or to kiss them from your salt stung cheeks
lacing your eyelashes with sorrowful jewels

So you read,
You pace,
You eat,
You pace some more
Then you sit
Just sit
The furniture drowns you
Everything seems larger or are you shrinking away?
Its hard to grasp at reality
Maybe it's a bad dream you'll wake up soon in someone's arms
Am I sleepwalking?
It's not real none of it is

Open your eyes
It is time to awaken
Spread your wings little Butterfly.

GUILT.

The light at the end of the tunnel
Drawing us Like bees to their hive
Is it there to sway us from our true path
Is it to be trusted
Or does truth lie in the darkness
Secrets told under the Ebony cloak
They spill from our lips unhindered
For Willing ears to behold
Whispers echoing amidst our twilight confidante
Our hopes our dreams Our unsavoury deeds
In the confession box
Un-judged
Our sins absolved
A clean slate
Making way for new sins and devilish behaviour
Utter rebellious deliciousness.

ANIMAM AGERE.

Thoughts of you fall like a blizzard of snow
Thick flurries that melt Almost as quick as they appear
All is but a precious memory when you're Coming undone
Unravelled
Dislocated

I still remember the pain

Push the blade into my chest
Plunge your hands into the space that you create
Take what is yours
As my blood flows through your fingers The sinful flavour swims on your
tongue
Taste my soul it is Tainted with lust

As I drift on this voyage to a place I know not

Terrors unite to control my dreams and Selene commands the tides
Night turns to day as I slip between worlds and my wounds melt away
Swirls of red vacate my scars
Crimson screams through the Onyx sky

The cool air cushions me through my descent
Back to the forest of thorns In which I am cut to ribbons
And once again the pain pleases me so

Death rattle echoes through the Treacherous dark
The white rabbit blinded by Temptations Wrath halts deep within the
cuniculus
He breathes me in
His eyes a cloud of grey and white seeking me out in his perpetual
blackness
Sanguine tears stain his fur
As he mourns my death and tastes this fruitless life upon his lips

And for you my love I have given my last breath.

AMARE

It's just like a dream A surreal imaginary land

Love

Where nothing feels real Yet everything is whole
And the truth is set free
Where all others are forsaken
As if there are only two souls in the galaxy Proxima Centauri and beyond
And kisses are as pure as the first snow
more exquisite than all the gems of this earth combined
Rarer than Painite
It's warmth thaws the iciest of places
Lighting the darkest depths unfathomable leagues deep
And the lust is salacious

Insatiable..

Like fine fragrance top notes of rose and iris
Base notes of night jasmine
Nuances of peonies

Bottle it and treasure it.

MEADOWS SONG

Lay me down on the grassy bank
Rolling hills awash with lush greens
As far as the eye can see
I smell your scent upon the wind as if you are here with me
Apricating in the solar glow
Helios blesses me with his heat

I feel your hand in mine
Clasping me tight
Our fingers lock with invisible twine
Skylarks scatter across the unending sky
Cerulean blue speckled with black
I see your face in the clouds it makes me smile
Cumulonimbus drift with the breeze as if on a journey to New lands
I close my eyes amidst the meadow blooms
The mellifluous sound of crickets singing in the tall grass

My chest rising and falling to the rhythm of nature and the beating of
hearts
Both mine and the little creatures of the earth
Nature is not saddened by the discontent of mortals
She whispers hope

Always

The intensity of your kiss I feel it on my lips
Urgent,
fervent
Almost like it was yesterday

I can still taste you.

HECATES PROMISE

The oceans of time that kept us apart
Now a mere drop of dew on the tip of a forest fern
The world could be in ruin
Cities swept away by the typhoons of Poseidons Wrath

I will find you

Your love a beacon in the dark
Ultraviolet.
Bridges stretching out across deep chasms burned to cinders

I will reach the other side

Not even Hades himself could halt my path
His fire may rain upon me the heat scoring my flesh
It shall not deter a Goddess kissed by the flame of her heart
Unbreakable bonds no sword could separate

My immortal soul will find you in this life and the next.

SPELLBOUND

I am under your spell

Dark magik Conjured by my one true love
I yearn to feel Your flesh upon mine
The coolness of claret drenched satin
Your scent upon my skin for all eternity
the alluring warmth of burnt wood and clove

Oh to gaze into those eyes, deep dark pools of hypnotic liquor
I could drown in them and get love drunk all at once,
Lost forever
Like ill fated ships finding Thonis Heracleion

To taste your life force upon my lips
Rose red kisses
I crave you like a drug
Don't drip feed me I want all of you,
Every last bit

And in return i'll give you all of me.

DEATH TO THE FLEDGLING HEART

Destined to be abandoned by thee
Fated to drift upon this sea
Deep and black with hues of blue
Oh how I loved the bones of you

secrets carried upon a sigh
Shattered dreams of you and I
Your flameless soul could never comply
 I cut the strings and let you fly

You let me drown in naked tears
Suffocated by wretched fears
I'd do anything to keep you near
Destroy the ones that you hold dear

Your Piercing eyes uncover my disguise Laying me bare
Quickening my demise
 I tried to live with devious lies
My love for you could part the skies

I take this dagger your blood entwined
and pierce the heart that once was mine
An endless sleep in crimson wine
Thus committing this mortal crime
I couldn't exist another moment
Echoing in this silence so peacefully fluent

With the pain of this love and my Treacherous heart
Upon this wave our souls shall part.

EPYLLION

Your lips kiss my fair brow
To the tip of my nose to my cupids bow
With violent emotion
As you turn me inside out and upside down In the best way
Your eyes intensely pierce the last layer of the veil i so fiercely used to
Protect myself
They burn into my soul in ways I cannot describe
Your hands treat me with such care As if I were something precious
A tiny wrens egg waiting to hatch
Holding the beating life within your palms
Cracks show where I have been damaged
Yet out of anyone I have ever known I trust you to not drop or shatter me

I let myself go

Your fingers clasp mine as you lead me on intrepid adventures
Leaving footprints in the sand
And fashioning Hearts out of damaged shells
The type no one else wants

The beauty of missing pieces

White and grey against the pearlescent ochre canvas
With great tenderness and strength you are Hero's Leander
And because maybe you do not hear it enough
You are a miraculous being full of golden spun sunshine with a wild heart
Just like mine

We are reflections in each others mirrors when all around us are cold stone
Walls
Take my hand, kiss me deep
Let us travel to unchartered shores
Where we can curl around each others soft naked bodies
As our hammock sways gently to the beat of our hearts.

Printed in Great Britain
by Amazon

21928082R00036